Deena
the Diwali Fairy

Join the **Rainbow Magic Reading Challenge!**

Read the story and collect your fairy points to climb the Reading Rainbow at the back of the book.

This book is worth 1 star.

To Isla, who is full of light and joy

Special thanks to Rachel Elliot
With thanks to Inclusive Minds
for connecting us with their
Inclusion Ambassador network, and in
particular to Zainab M Ahmad
for their input

ORCHARD BOOKS

First published in Great Britain in 2020 by The Watts Publishing Group

1 3 5 7 9 10 8 6 4 2

HiT entertainment

© 2020 Rainbow Magic Limited
© 2020 HIT Entertainment Limited
Illustrations © 2020 The Watts Publishing Group Limited

A CIP catalogue record for this book is available from the British Library.

ISBN 978 1 40836 234 1

Printed and bound in Great Britain by Clays Ltd, Elcograf S.p.A.

MIX
Paper from
responsible sources
FSC® C104740

The paper and board used in this book are made from wood from responsible sources

Orchard Books
An imprint of Hachette Children's Group
Part of The Watts Publishing Group Limited
Carmelite House, 50 Victoria Embankment, London EC4Y 0DZ

An Hachette UK Company
www.hachette.co.uk
www.hachettechildrens.co.uk

Deena
the Diwali
Fairy

By Daisy Meadows

ORCHARD

www.rainbowmagicbooks.co.uk

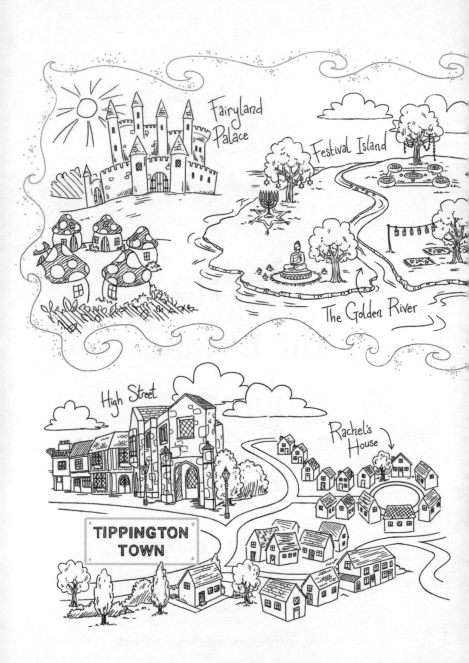

Jack Frost's
Ice Castle

Jack Frost's Festival Tent

WETHERBURY

Kirsty's House

Jack Frost's Spell

Ignore Eid and Buddha Day.
Make Diwali go away.
Scrap Hanukkah and make them see –
They should be celebrating me!

I'll steal ideas and spoil their fun.
My Frost Day plans have just begun.
Bring gifts and sweets to celebrate
The many reasons I'm so great!

Contents

Chapter One
An Unexpected Invitation

It was teatime in late October.
Wetherbury village had already settled
down for the night. Every house had
its lights glowing and its curtains shut.
A blustery wind whirled russet leaves
along the pavements. Thick, heavy clouds
scudded across the sky.

"The clouds are pressed together as if they can't bear to be apart," said Kirsty Tate, her nose pressed up against the sitting-room window.

"Just like us," said her best friend, Rachel Walker.

The girls shared a happy smile. Rachel had come to stay for the weekend, and they were looking forward to having lots of fun.

"I wonder if we'll see any of our fairy friends," said Kirsty. "Adventures always seem to happen when we're together."

Magic had been a part of their friendship from the beginning. When they first met, they had been plunged into an exciting mission to save the Rainbow Fairies from Jack Frost and his naughty goblins. Ever since, they had helped the fairies many times.

"Someone's coming to your house," said Rachel, pressing her nose against the window too.

A lady in a glittering sari was walking up the path.

"That's our new neighbour, Mrs Anand," said Kirsty. "She moved in last month."

The doorbell rang, and they heard Mr Tate go to the door.

"Does she have children?" Rachel asked.

"Yes, a boy called Kirin," said Kirsty. "He's in my class at school."

Just then, Mr Tate called them. They found him standing next to Mrs Anand, beaming at them.

"Mrs Anand has come with a very special invitation for you both," he said.

"This week, Kirin and I are celebrating Diwali," said Mrs Anand. "It's the Hindu festival of lights. Today is the main day of the festival, and we're having a party. I'm inviting a few of Kirin's classmates and

their parents to join us. Would you like to come?"

"Yes please," said Kirsty.

"That sounds lovely," said Rachel.

"Come over now if you like," said Mrs Anand. "You can help Kirin with the decorating, and he can tell you a bit more about Diwali."

Soon, the girls were gazing up at Mrs Anand's house.

"I've never seen it looking like this before," said Kirsty.

Ropes of golden lights hung from the walls. Multi-coloured curtains were draped in every window, and the front door was decorated with embroidered door hangings.

"Those door hangings are toran," said Mrs Anand. "And these flower patterns on the hall floor are called rangoli. They are symbols of good luck and prosperity to all who enter our home."

"They look as if they're made from petals," said Rachel.

"So they are," said Mrs Anand. "They're meant to show strength and bring good luck."

"What about all these pretty lamps?" asked Kirsty, pointing at rows of oil lamps flickering like tiny candles around

the front door.

"They're diyas," said Mrs Anand. "Aren't they lovely?"

A boy appeared at the top of the stairs.

"Hi Kirin," said Kirsty.

"Hi," he replied. "I'm glad you came. Is this Rachel? I've heard loads about you."

"Thanks for inviting me too," said Rachel. "I've heard about Diwali at school but I don't know much about it."

"Come up and I'll explain while I finish decorating the attic," he said.

The girls had to go carefully up the stairs, because there were strings of paper flowers on every step, each one a different colour. Kirin led them up a narrow little staircase to the attic.

"Will you help me hang some more lights across the window?" he asked.

"Mum loves everywhere to be lit up for the party."

He held up a string of lanterns, and the girls helped as he hooked them up around the room.

"Diwali lasts for five days, but today is the most important one," said Kirin. "It's the day of light, when Hindus celebrate the triumph of good over bad."

"So that's why there are lights everywhere," said Kirsty.

"Not just lights," said Kirin, giving her a sideways grin. "There will be fireworks later, and mithai — the best sweets you ever tasted."

"Kirin, more of your guests have arrived," Mrs Anand called.

"We'll finish this," said Rachel.

"Are you sure?" said Kirin. "Thanks,

both of you. See you downstairs!"

He bounded out of the attic. As Rachel and Kirsty hooked the last lanterns across the window, they started to glow.

"Did you turn on the switch?" asked Rachel.

Kirsty shook her head.

"Neither did I," Rachel said. "That's a magical glow!"

One lantern was shining brighter than the rest. Each of its sides was made of differently coloured glass. The orange side clicked open, and a fairy leaned out.

"Quickly," she said, beckoning to them. "I need your help!"

Chapter Two
Frost Day

The fairy threw a handful of sparkling fairy dust out of the lantern. As soon as it touched Rachel and Kirsty, they dwindled down to fairy size. Lacy wings unfurled and lifted them into the air. With fairy dust glittering around them, they fluttered into the lantern.

"I'm Deena the Diwali Fairy," said the little fairy.

She was wearing a long purple and pink dress with a gold sun pattern across the bottom.

"Have you come to celebrate with Kirin and his mum?" Kirsty asked.

Deena shook her head.

"I wish I had," she said in a worried voice. "There's something wrong in Fairyland. Please will you come and help?"

"Of course we will," said Rachel.

With a flick of Deena's wand, the tiny orange lantern door clicked shut. Suddenly, everything went dark. Coloured lights flickered high and low, left and right. Rachel and Kirsty blinked and rubbed their eyes. Then the lantern door swung open.

"Welcome back to Fairyland," said Deena.

Stars were twinkling overhead. Rachel and Kirsty stepped out on to a white marble floor, decorated with bright rangoli. There were colourful beanbags at each corner, and red toran were hanging from the trees around them. Spices, perfumes and incense made the air sweet.

"What a beautiful place," said Kirsty.

"I can hear running water," said
Rachel.

"Look behind you," said Deena,
stepping out beside them.

Rachel and Kirsty turned, and saw
a river gurgling and splashing its way
among the trees. Rows of diyas flickered
and floated on the surface.

"That's the Golden River," said Deena.

"I've never seen this part of Fairyland before," said Kirsty. "Where are we?"

"This is Festival Island," said Deena. "Here, the Festival Fairies make sure every human festival is happy and successful."

"Is it always this quiet?' Rachel asked. Deena shook her head.

"Usually the river is lined with fairies,"

she said. "But I warned them not to come. Something is sure to go wrong."

"But we're in the middle of Diwali," said Kirsty. "Isn't this the most important day of the festival?"

"It should be," Deena replied. "But because of Jack Frost, everything has changed."

Just then three fairies zoomed towards them through the trees.

"You're here!" they called out. "Welcome!"

"I'd like to introduce Hana the Hanukkah Fairy, Elisha the Eid Fairy and Bea the Buddha Day Fairy," said Deena. "We're the Festival Fairies."

"It's lovely to meet you," said Rachel. "Deena said that you need us."

"Queen Titania said we should fetch

you," said Hana. "She told us about all the things you've done to help Fairyland, and we're hoping that you might help us too."

"Tell us what happened," said Kirsty.

"We were making mithai with Deena

when we had a visit from Jack Frost," said Bea. "He arrived shouting orders at us."

"What sort of orders?" Rachel asked.

"Let me show you," said Deena.

She raised her wand and waved it as if she were drawing a rangoli. The flower shape hung in the air in glimmering golden fairy dust, and a picture formed inside it. Rachel and Kirsty saw Jack Frost standing on the marble floor in daylight, with his hands on his hips. The Festival Fairies were standing in front of him.

"Do you know how amazing I am?" he boasted. "I'm the best. I make everyone else look stupid. So why don't I have a festival? Those stupid humans celebrate everything. They're celebrating light, for

crying out loud.
Everyone should
be celebrating
me."

"They celebrate
light in the heart
of winter," said
Deena in her
gentle voice. "It
makes them feel
bright and happy.
It reminds them
that kindness and
goodness will
always win."

"Fiddlesticks,"
said Jack Frost.
"There should
be a festival to

celebrate me. I'm going to call it Frost
Day. I've spent a lot of time thinking
about this."

"How long?" asked Elisha.

"Ten whole minutes!" Jack Frost
boasted. "I thought of two brilliant ideas
for the festival. Everyone will have to
wear icicle costumes and eat freezing
food. Now you can do the rest and make
it all happen."

He wiggled his bony fingers. The
Festival Fairies exchanged a glance with
each other.

"We can help you," said Deena. "But it
was your idea, and you should do most
of the work."

Jack Frost's eyes nearly popped out of
his head.

"Me?" he exclaimed. "Me . . . work?

How dare you?"

"We can't just make a festival for you," said Elisha.

"Gobbledygook!" Jack Frost yelled. "Drivel, gibberish and twaddle! You're the Festival Fairies – do what I say. Use all the best ideas from your festivals and turn them into Frost Day!"

"Listen," said Bea, putting her hand on his arm. "It's wrong to steal ideas from other people."

"They're right," said Deena. "You have to think of your own ideas. That's the only way to make Frost Day unique."

Jack Frost stamped his foot, and his spiky beard quivered.

"Do what I tell you!" he shrieked as loud as he could.

When the fairies shook their heads, he

stormed away from them, clenching his fists in frustration.

"I'll make you sorry!" he yelled over his shoulder.

Chapter Three
Festival Tent

"What happened next?" asked Rachel. Deena waved her wand again. The picture faded, and a new image took its place. This time it showed goblins on the marble floor. There were goblins rolling over the rangoli, goblins hanging from the toran and goblins dangling from the glass lanterns that were strung between the trees.

"This is what we found when we arrived the next morning," said Deena. "We keep our magical objects in those lanterns."

"What are your magical objects?" Rachel asked.

"Deena's diya, Hana's hanukkiah, Elisha's Eid candle and my Buddha candle," said Bea. "They help us make the special magic that looks after the festivals."

SMASH! The goblins shattered the glass lanterns. Screeching with laughter, they snatched the magical objects.

"Bring those back!" cried Deena.

"No way!" squawked the goblins. "They're ours now."

"Jack Frost sent us to help make Frost Day special," said the tallest one.

"Stealing doesn't make anything special," said Hana. "It just spoils things. Besides, the magical objects only work near the festival time."

"Frost Day is going to happen every year," the tall goblin shouted.

Before the fairies could do anything, the goblins had leapt past them and vanished among the trees.

Deena waved her wand, and the picture vanished.

"They took our things to Jack Frost so that he could develop Frost Day," she said. "Without them, we can't look after any of the festivals."

"The festivals are spread out through the year," said Bea. "The three of us have a bit of time to try to find our objects, but Deena's right in the middle of Diwali."

"Every Diwali celebration is going to be a disaster," said Deena, sinking down on to a purple beanbag. "Without my diya, I can't make sure that all the traditions, decorations and celebrations are perfect."

She buried her face in her hands. Rachel and Kirsty rushed to her side.

"We came to help," Rachel reminded her. "We can get your diya back."

"It's too late," Deena said in a muffled voice. "I brought you to help the others. Jack Frost has spoiled Diwali."

"Don't give up," said Kirsty. "We can stop Jack Frost."

"And the first place we should look is

the Ice Castle," Rachel added.

"Let's all go," said Hana.

But Deena shook her head.

"The fewer of us, the better," she said. "If we're captured, we'll need your help."

"Then we'll stay here and watch over the island," said Bea. "Good luck, all of you."

Deena, Rachel and Kirsty rose into

the air. Fluttering over the treetops, they could see that they had been on an island in the middle of a silvery sea. In the distance, the waves were breaking on the sandy beaches of Fairyland.

"Jack Frost's Castle, here we come," said Deena.

The three fairies swooped towards the coastline, zipping across the blue sky. They passed over flowery meadows and toadstool houses, but soon the weather began to change. Dark grey clouds loomed overhead, and their faces were prickled with specks of hail. Shivering, Kirsty pointed to the towers of the Ice Castle ahead.

"We're nearly there," she said.

"I can't see any goblin guards," she said. "We should be able to get in through the trapdoor on the battlements."

"How do you know about the trapdoor?" asked Deena as they landed on top of the castle.

"Past adventures," said Rachel, smiling at her.

She bent down to open the secret way in, but Kirsty stopped her and leaned over the battlements, peering into the gardens.

"What's that?" she asked.

The gardens were hidden under a canopy of blue and silver.

"It looks like a circus big top," said Rachel.

"Or a festival tent," said Deena. "Let's find out."

They fluttered down from the battlements and landed behind the enormous tent. From inside, they could hear the squawks of goblins and the roaring voice of Jack Frost. Slowly, Rachel tucked up her wings and lifted the back of the tent. She crawled through the gap.

"It's OK," she whispered. "Come on."

Inside, there were rangoli made from blue and silver flowers on the floor, all in the shape of Jack Frost's face. Jack Frost was sitting on a velvet, embroidered throne.

"That's the most amazing embroidery I've ever seen," said Deena. "He must

have used my magical diya to create all this. He's going to steal from Diwali to make Frost Day happen."

"How can stealing ideas spoil the real Diwali?" Kirsty asked.

"Because while he has the magical

diya, the ideas he uses will stop working in the human world," said Deena. "Diyas won't light, rangoli will break up and mithai will taste horrible. He's going to spoil everything."

Chapter Four
City Celebrations

Jack Frost clicked his fingers and three goblins ran towards him.

"Frost Day is going to be bigger than Christmas," he announced.

"But when is Frost Day?" whinged the smallest goblin. "I'm hungry."

"I'm bored," wailed another.

"I'm tired," said the third goblin.

"I need more ideas," said Jack Frost, stamping his foot. "What's the use of the stupid magical diya if it doesn't do all the thinking for me? Give me ideas now."

The goblins exchanged alarmed looks. There was a long silence.

"You could turn the tent into a big trampoline," said the smallest goblin. "It could be a bouncing festival, with ice cream."

"I'm not a kangaroo!" Jack Frost yelled. "You're all useless. I'm going to steal some more ideas from a real Diwali celebration. And you're coming with me."

He jabbed the shoulder of the smallest goblin, who squeaked in surprise. There was a flash of blue lightning, and Jack Frost and the goblin vanished from the festival tent.

"He's gone to spoil someone's Diwali," said Rachel. "Can you follow him, Deena?"

Deena nodded and whirled her wand in a circle around them.

"Like a firework's starry tail
Help us chase the lightning trail."

WHOOSH! The three fairies spun
around and zoomed through a blur
of golden light. Blinking, they found
themselves sitting on a marble staircase in
a grand house. They were still tiny fairies,
and each of them was sitting inside a
paper flower on the stairs.

"Where are we?" asked Kirsty.

"This is the biggest Diwali party in the
city," said Deena. "I come here every year
to make sure that everything is perfect."

Fireworks were exploding in the garden.
Waiters and waitresses were gliding
around with trays of food and drinks.
Everyone was wearing bright colours,
and the clothes were decorated with tiny

mirrors. They glimmered in the light from
the diyas.

"Wow, there are a lot of guests at this
party," said Kirsty.

"But is he here?" asked Deena.

Jack Frost's brash voice rose over the hum of friendly conversation.

"Give me that," he was demanding. "I want more of those. What's this for?"

The fairies slipped out of their paper

flowers and flew low, dodging through the crowd.

"There he is," said Rachel.

The Ice Lord was elbowing people out of the way, snatching at the food, drink and decorations. One goblin was behind him, wearing a cap decorated with light bulbs and a long coat dotted with tiny mirrors. Jack Frost picked up a string of paper flowers and put it around his neck.

"Add this to my ideas," he said, throwing another string to the goblin. "Paper flower necklaces! What a marvellous idea of mine. My, my, how brilliant I am. Sometimes I amaze myself."

"Look at all the other flowers," said Kirsty.

One by one, the paper flowers that decorated the stairs and windowsills fell apart. The fairies flew up high and perched on a bookshelf. Below them, Jack Frost was stuffing mithai into his mouth.

"Yum, I want lots of these at my festival," he muttered. "Magic lamp, make it happen."

"Look at his pocket," said Rachel.

Something inside his cape pocket was glowing. Deena gasped. "I think that's my diya," she said. "I can see its shape."

"Now we just have to get it out of his pocket," said Kirsty.

"Why is it glowing?" Rachel asked.

"It's glowing because he's using its magic," said Deena. "Jack Frost wants paper flowers and mithai, so he's taken them all. The ones in the human world will be ruined."

"Yuck!" exclaimed a little boy, spitting his sweet into his hand.

His mother started to tell him off, and the three fairies exchanged a knowing glance. Just then, Jack Frost spotted a row of diyas.

"Those!" he yelled, making the goblin next to him jump. "I want lots and lots of those."

The diyas went out instantly, and his cape pocket glowed even more brightly.

"Mine!" Jack Frost said, gloating.

As he walked around the house, every diya he passed flickered and went out. People exclaimed and groaned as the house grew darker.

"Ha ha, got you!" said Jack Frost to each one. "The little lights are all mine."

He cackled and rubbed his hands

together, greedily.

"Diwali is the Festival of Lights," said Deena, clasping her hands together. "Without the diya flames, Diwali will have no meaning."

Chapter Five
Super Sunglasses

After a few minutes, all the flames had gone out. Jack Frost ran out of the door and capered along the pavement towards the next house. The goblin skipped along beside him, and the fairies flew behind.

"I'm glad it's night-time," whispered Rachel. "No one will see us."

"Especially if Jack Frost keeps stealing their lights," added Kirsty. "Let's try to sneak up to him while he's looking at the decoration. Maybe we can slip the magical diya away from him."

The goblin giggled as Jack Frost knocked on the door of the next Diwali-decorated house.

"Let me in," he said to the surprised owners. "I'm here for the party."

He bounded inside and started looking around. The fairies flew in above, staying close to the ceiling. In the back garden, several children were waving colourful sparklers.

"Get me some of those," Jack Frost told the goblin.

"Those sparklers are called phuljhari," said Deena. "They're a tradition at

Diwali parties."

The goblin handed a packet to his
master, and he tucked it into his cape.

"Look at all the other phuljhari," said
Rachel.

Some of the children were crying
because their sparklers had failed to light.
Others had suddenly gone out.

"I need more light," Jack Frost said.

He bent over the diyas and laughed as they went out. Around him, the guests groaned.

"Why do all those humans look sad?" asked the goblin.

"Who cares?" said Jack Frost. "I want more lights. More!"

The electric lights went out and the house was plunged into darkness. Jack Frost moved on to the next decorated house.

"He's being so mean," said Deena. "People are inviting him in to be friendly, and he's taking away all the joy of Diwali."

"We have to stop him," said Kirsty. "I don't want him to spoil Mrs Anand's party back in Wetherbury."

By the time they reached the end of the

street, every house that was celebrating Diwali had gone dark. Deena's magical diya was so bright that it was like daylight. Jack Frost wasn't laughing any more. The fairies fluttered down behind the nearest street sign.

"It hurts my eyes," they heard the goblin wail. "I want to go home to Goblin Grotto where it's nice and dark."

"Shut up," snapped Jack Frost.

"Can't you put it in your pocket?" the goblin grumbled.

"No," Jack Frost shouted. "I don't want my cape to be lit up like a firework."

From behind the street sign, Rachel, Kirsty and Deena could hear every word.

"We can't sneak up and get my magical diya back now," said Deena. "With all this light, Jack Frost will be sure to see us coming."

"If only we could blindfold him," said Rachel.

"You've given me an idea," said Kirsty. "He would never let us blindfold him, but there is another way. Deena, can you make us human sized again and disguise us?"

"Yes, I can disguise you in a twinkling," said Deena, holding up her wand. "But what sort of disguise do you want?"

Kirsty smiled.

"Sunglasses sellers," she said. "We have to get him to try on some special sunglasses. They'll make everything go dark, and that's when you swoop in."

Deena waved her wand and fairy dust shimmered all around them. As soon as it touched Rachel and Kirsty, their wings vanished and they grew back to human size.

"Oh my goodness, we look so funny," said Kirsty, spluttering with laughter.

The girls were wearing white suits decorated with a black sunglasses pattern. Their hair was slicked back in tight

ponytails, and each of them was wearing sunglasses.

"Do you think Jack Frost will recognise us?" Rachel asked.

"No way," said Deena. "I hardly recognise you! Just get him to put these on."

She handed each of them a pair of large sunglasses shaped like snowflakes. Feeling a bit nervous, the girls strode towards Jack Frost and the goblin. Their sunglasses dimmed the light, but they could still see.

"Wow, your light is super bright," said Kirsty.

"I know that," said Jack Frost, glaring at her. "Who are you?"

"We're the Super Sunglasses team," said Rachel. "We're looking for customers. Do you know anyone who might like some sunglasses?"

"Me!" squeaked the goblin.

Jack Frost shoved him out of the way and held out his hand.

"Give me your darkest pair," he growled.

"Certainly, sir," said Kirsty in a cheerful

voice. "Try these."

She handed him the snowflake sunglasses. Rachel reached into her bag and picked out a pair for the goblin too.

"I bet these will make me look brainy," he said, putting them on.

Still holding the diya in one hand, Jack Frost put the snowflake sunglasses on.

"Ahh, that's better," he said. "I can't see any light at all."

Rachel glanced over her shoulder at Deena and nodded. Deena darted towards Jack Frost's hand, but his long, bony fingers were clasped around the diya. Deena looked at the girls in a panic. What now?

Chapter Six
Magic and Mithai

"Would you mind holding up your lamp so I can see something?" Kirsty asked.

Jack Frost grunted and raised his hand. His fingers uncurled and Deena dived towards the diya.

"Actually, I can't see anything," said Jack Frost.

He raised his other hand to tear the glasses off – just as Deena flung her arms around the diya. Instantly it shrank to fairy size, and she zoomed into the sky with it.

"Bring that back!" Jack Frost hollered, shaking his fist at her.

Deena shook her head and tapped the diya with her wand. Its light faded, and Rachel nudged Kirsty and pointed along the street. They could see the flicker of hundreds of tiny lanterns outside the houses.

"The lights have come back," Kirsty said in delight. "Hurray!"

Jack Frost turned to glare at her.

"This is nothing to do with you," he snapped.

"It's everything to do with them," said Deena from above. "They have saved Diwali."

She pointed her wand, and their disguises disappeared. Jack Frost's eyes narrowed, and his spiky beard quivered.

"I'll get you back for this," he hissed, pointing his finger at them. "I've still got three magical objects, and the next festival will give me everything I need for Frost Day."

He stamped his foot, and he and the goblin disappeared with a deafening clap of thunder. Deena flew down and perched on Rachel's hand.

"Thank you both," she said. "You have made sure that Diwali will be a success for Hindus all around the human world."

"We want to help find the other objects too," said Rachel.

"I know that Bea, Elisha and Hana will be glad of your help," said Deena. "But it may take many months to find them. You see, the festivals are spread out through the year, and each object's magic will only start to work near the time. Jack Frost is bound to keep them hidden until then."

"We don't mind how long it takes," said Kirsty. "We'll be ready whenever any of

the Festival Fairies needs us."

"Thank you,' said Deena. "Knowing that we have your help has given us all hope. And now it is time for you to celebrate the joy of Diwali. Enjoy the party, my friends!"

She waved her wand, and Rachel and Kirsty were swept up in a dizzy, magical

rush of golden twinkles. Seconds later,
they were once again standing in the
attic at Mrs Anand's house. Hand in
hand, they hurried down the stairs and
met Kirin on his way up.

"I was just coming to find you," he said.

"Thanks for sorting out the lanterns. I've saved some of the best mithai for you."

He held out a plate and the girls each took a silver sweet.

"Yummy!" said Kirsty.

"Scrummy!" Rachel agreed.

Kirin looked pleased.

"Did you notice the lights go out earlier?" he asked as he led them downstairs. "Mum said it must have been a power cut because of the wind."

Rachel and Kirsty exchanged a secret smile. They knew what had made the lights go out – and what had turned them on again. There were still three magical objects to find and the Festival Fairies were going to need their help. But for now, they could relax and enjoy the party.

"I wonder what the next festival adventure will be," Rachel whispered as they followed Kirin down.

"I can't wait to find out," said Kirsty. "Happy Diwali, Rachel!"

The End

Now it's time for Kirsty and
Rachel to help…

Hana the Hanukkah Fairy

Read on for a sneak peek…

"Five snow fairies," said Rachel Walker in
a delighted voice. "This is the most snow
we've ever had in Tippington."

Her best friend, Kirsty Tate, rubbed the
snow off her mittens and smiled. She had
come to stay with Rachel after the end
of the autumn term. They had spent all
afternoon building the snow fairies, and
it was starting to get dark.

"I wish they were real," she said.

Being together again had given them
a chance to talk about their most recent
adventure in Fairyland. Jack Frost had
stolen the magical objects that belonged

to the Festival Fairies. He was planning his own festival, which he called Frost Day, and he wanted to steal as many ideas he could from Diwali, Hanukkah, Eid and Buddha Day.

Rachel and Kirsty had helped Deena the Diwali Fairy to get her diya back, but there were still three magical objects missing, and three other fairies whose festivals were in danger.

"I really thought we'd have a visit from Hana the Hanukkah Fairy," said Rachel.

Hanukkah, the Jewish Festival of Light, was nearly over, and they hadn't seen a single speck of magic. The girls didn't know when – or if – Hana would need them.

The back door opened, and Mr Walker came out carrying a box.

"Girls, would you take this over to Abigail's house?" he said. "I promised her dad I'd make some doughnuts for their Hanukkah celebrations tonight. They said you could stay for the ceremony if you like."

"Yes please," said Rachel.

"What kind of doughnuts?" said Kirsty, peeping into box. "Oh, jam. Yum!"

"In Hebrew, they are called 'sufganiyot'," said Mr Walker. "I believe that there are all sorts of delicious things to eat at a Hanukkah party."

Eagerly, the girls took the box and walked down the street. Snow started to fall again.

"Is Abigail in your class?" Kirsty asked.

"No, she goes to a different school," said Rachel. "But our dads are friends, so we play together sometimes."

Abigail lived in a tall, red-brick house on the corner of the street. Rachel and Kirsty ran up the steps and knocked on the green wooden door. They heard running footsteps, and then the door was flung open by a slim girl with bobbed black hair.

Read *Hana the Hanukkah Fairy* to find out what adventures are in store for Kirsty and Rachel!

Calling all parents, carers and teachers!
The Rainbow Magic fairies are here to help
your child enter the magical world of reading.
Whatever reading stage they are at, there's
a Rainbow Magic book for everyone!
Here is Lydia the Reading Fairy's guide to
supporting your child's journey at all levels.

(1)

Starting Out
Our Rainbow Magic Beginner Readers are perfect for first-time readers who are just beginning to develop reading skills and confidence. Approved by teachers, they contain a full range of educational levelling, as well as lively full-colour illustrations.

(2)

Developing Readers
Rainbow Magic Early Readers contain longer stories and wider vocabulary for building stamina and growing confidence. These are adaptations of our most popular Rainbow Magic stories, specially developed for younger readers in conjunction with an Early Years reading consultant, with full-colour illustrations.

(3)

Going Solo
The Rainbow Magic chapter books – a mixture of series and one-off specials – contain accessible writing to encourage your child to venture into reading independently. These highly collectible and much-loved magical stories inspire a love of reading to last a lifetime.

www.rainbowmagicbooks.co.uk

"Rainbow Magic got my daughter reading chapter books. Great sparkly covers, cute fairies and traditional stories full of magic that she found impossible to put down" – Mother of Edie (6 years)

"Florence LOVES the Rainbow Magic books. She really enjoys reading now" – Mother of Florence (6 years)

Read along the Reading Rainbow!

Well done – you have completed the book!

This book was worth 1 star.

See how far you have climbed on the Reading Rainbow opposite.
The more books you read, the more stars you can colour in
and the closer you will be to becoming a Royal Fairy!

Do you want to print your own Reading Rainbow?

1) Go to the Rainbow Magic website

2) Download and print out the poster

3) Colour in a star for every book you finish
and climb the Reading Rainbow

4) For every step up the rainbow,
you can download your very own certificate

There's all this and lots more at
rainbowmagicbooks.co.uk

You'll find activities, stories, a special newsletter
AND you can search for the fairy with your name!